P9-DWK-610

Go on all the MYSTIC KNIGHTS adventures:

Book #1

The Legend of the Ancient Scroll

Written by Michael Teitelbaum

HarperEntertainment
A Division of HarperCollinsPublishers

♦HarperEntertainment

A Division of HarperCollins*Publishers*
10 East 53rd Street, New York, NY 10022-5299

This is a work of fiction. The characters, incidents, and dialogues
are products of the author's imagination, or if real, are used ficti-
tiously. Any resemblance to actual events or persons, living or
dead, is entirely coincidental.

First printing: May 1999

Cover illustration by Mel Grant
Designed by Susan Sanguily

Printed in the United States of America
ISBN 0–06–107160–9

HarperCollins®, ♦ ®, and HarperEntertainment™ are
trademarks of HarperCollins Publishers Inc.

Visit HarperEntertainment on the World Wide Web at
http://www.harpercollins.com

10 9 8 7 6 5 4 3 2

Welcome, Great Seer

You, dear reader, are a powerful, mystical being known as the Great Seer of Tir na Nog. You can witness and control the fate of the four brave heroes in this story. This wondrous magical gift has always been within you. At several points in this tale you will be asked to make a choice . . . a choice that will affect the lives of not only Rohan, Ivar, Deirdre, and Angus, but also the entire kingdom. They need the guidance of your mystical powers.

But with great power comes great responsibility. So, Great Seer, use your gift wisely. For the destiny of the Mystic Knights of Tir na Nog—and the fate of the Kingdom of Kells—rests in your mighty hands!

History

Long ago, far across oceans, an island was divided into two kingdoms. The Kingdom of Kells was ruled by good King Conchobar. The Kingdom of Temra was ruled by the evil Queen Maeve. Queen Maeve believed that it was her birthright to rule the entire island. She would therefore not rest until her armies had conquered Kells.

King Conchobar's army fought fiercely, and the evil queen was stopped time and again. In desperation, Maeve turned to the dark magic of an evil fairy named Mider. Using the powers of sorcery given to her by Mider, Maeve conjured a host of terrible giants, ogres, and other mystical beasts to help her battle the armies of Kells. Aided by the creatures of darkness, Maeve's forces turned the tide of battle. It was a dark time for Kells, and King Conchobar even talked of surrender. All hope seemed lost . . .

But was it?

The king's trusted advisor, Cathbad the Druid, who possessed special powers, had raised an orphan named Rohan. Now eighteen and Cathbad's apprentice, Rohan had become a skilled swordsman. But Cathbad had never revealed to Rohan that there was an amazing secret about the young apprentice's destiny.

Cathbad had in his possession a piece of an Ancient Scroll that spoke of the coming of a great warrior named Draganta, who would bring peace to the land. Now, in these desperate times, Cathbad revealed the scroll to Rohan . . . and showed him that a birthmark on Rohan's arm matched a symbol on the scroll!

Upon seeing this, and learning of the prophecy of the coming of Draganta, Rohan was convinced that he was the one to lead the quest to find the legendary warrior—the Kingdom of Kells's only hope.

Rohan is joined by Deirdre, King Conchobar's strong and beautiful daughter; Angus, Rohan's best friend; and Ivar, a prince from a faraway land across the sea. Together they must journey to Tir na Nog, the land beneath the Earth, where the magical wee folk live. With the help of Fin Varra, the wise but tricky king of Tir na Nog, the four young warriors must prove their worth so that they can become the MYSTIC KNIGHTS OF TIR NA NOG!

Then, and only then, can they find the warrior Draganta and save the Kingdom of Kells.

Lexicon

APPRENTICE: One who is learning a trade or occupation.

ARSENAL: A supply of weapons.

BATTALION: A large number of organized troops.

CHALICE: A fancy cup.

CONJURE: To summon or create by magical powers.

CREVICE: A narrow opening or crack.

DESTINY: The way events will work out, beyond human control.

DRUID: One who practices mystical arts, particularly nature magic.

FATE: The force that creates events that will happen.

FRAY: A brawl or battle.

ILLUSION: An image without substance.

LEXICON: A list of words.

LINEAGE: The path of sons and daughters from a single, usually royal, ancestor.

MENTOR: A wise and trusted teacher.

MORTAL: A human being.

MYSTIC: Magical, sacred, or mysterious.

NECTAR: A delicious drink.

OMINOUS: Menacing or threatening.

PORTAL: A doorway, an entrance, or a gate.

PROPHECY: A prediction of the future.

QUEST: A journey to seek something.

RAMPAGE: Moving in a violent manner.

REALM: A kingdom.

REGAL: Acting like a king or queen.

ROGUE: A scoundrel or rascal.

RUNE STONE: A stone carved with a symbol of an ancient alphabet, sometimes with magical powers.

SATCHEL: A small bag, often having a shoulder strap.

SCEPTER: A staff held by a king or queen as a symbol of rulership, or a magical staff held by a wizard, sorcerer, or druid.

SCROLL: An ancient document written on rolled parchment.

SQUADRON: A group of two or more soldiers, especially soldiers on horseback.

STALACTITES: An icicle-shaped mineral deposit hanging from the roof of a cavern.

STALAGMITES: A cone-shaped mineral deposit built up on the floor of a cavern, formed from the dripping of mineral-rich water.

TRANSFORM: To change the appearance or shape of something.

The Legend of
the Ancient Scroll

The war between Kells and Temra dragged on. On a battlefield shrouded in mist, the clanging of swords and the cries of soldiers filled the air. Rumors of a peace treaty had spread throughout the land, but the soldiers were skeptical. The war had been raging for so long that hope for peace had long ago faded from the minds of the warriors now fighting desperately for their lives.

One young Kells soldier found himself face-to-face with a Temran warrior. *I must stop the evil Temran invaders at all cost*, thought the Kells soldier as he set himself in a battle stance, feet wide, sword at the ready.

The Temran warrior swung his sword toward the Kells soldier, who raised his arms and blocked the blow with his shield. The Kells soldier pivoted, spun to the right, then swung his steel sword at his enemy. As metal clashed against metal, the Kells soldier wondered, for the hundredth time that day, if this war would ever really end.

Turn to page 12

Later, alone in his magical chamber, Cathbad studied a tattered fragment of the Ancient Scroll.

"What's that, more magic?" asked Rohan, stepping into the chamber.

Cathbad glanced at his young apprentice, then turned back to the scroll in his hands. "I've kept this a secret from you, Rohan," said the druid. "But perhaps it's now time for you to know of it." He handed the scroll to Rohan.

The young man read aloud. "'A mortal without lineage, marked with the brand of destiny, shall discover the warrior Draganta, who shall save Kells and bring peace to the land for a hundred lifetimes.'"

"It is the Ancient Scroll the legends tell of," Cathbad stated.

"And you've kept it hidden?" asked Rohan in amazement.

"The scroll is incomplete, and therefore dangerous," explained Cathbad. "It may release evil forces. I would not even bring it out now except that the situation in Kells is so desperate." Then he paused and spoke softly. "Rohan, do you remember when I found you?"

Rohan's mind drifted back to the day that he met the man who would become his mentor, teacher, guardian, and friend. "Of course," replied Rohan. "You came upon me as a group of children were throwing rocks and sticks at me. You thought they were being cruel to me, but actually I was swatting the rocks and sticks away with this." Rohan pulled out his old, rusty sword. "I was practicing to be a warrior."

"What else do you remember?" asked Cathbad.

"You asked me what I knew of this birthmark on my arm," recalled Rohan, pointing to the two curving red lines that formed the mark. "And you asked me who my parents were and where I came from. I knew neither answer, and nothing of the mark. All I knew of my past was this sword I carried, and still carry. Then you told me that the birthmark could link me to a great destiny, and asked me to become your apprentice until that destiny called."

Cathbad nodded. He held the scroll up next to Rohan's birthmark. A mark on the scroll was identical to the birthmark on Rohan's arm.

"My destiny," said Rohan in amazement, staring at the two marks. He took the scroll from Cathbad's hands. "I am that mortal without lineage who is destined to discover the warrior Draganta and save the people of Kells. *This* is my destiny!"

"You are inexperienced, Rohan," cautioned Cathbad. "Maeve will use all her dark powers to stop you."

Rohan set his jaw firmly. He slid his sword back into its sheath. "I am not afraid," he announced.

"Then let us inform the king," Cathbad said.

Turn to page 56

"Of all the wonders!" exclaimed Rohan. "My armor! This can surely aid me in my battle with this terrible Ogre!"

Rohan rushed over to the armor. He reached out to take it.

But his fingers passed right through the armor. It was only an illusion.

Before Rohan could react, he was instantly transported to a pit filled with phookas—goblins with the bodies of men and the heads of goats.

Maeve's evil laughter filled the air.

"By Daghda, I've been tricked!" Rohan shouted. "This was more of Maeve's dark magic. The image of the armor was just a trigger for the evil queen's treacherous trap."

Rohan swiftly pulled out his sword and prepared to shoot its blazing burst of flames at the vile creatures surrounding him. But before he could unleash the fiery fury, four phookas attacked him from behind. The enchanted Sword of Kells flew from his hand and Rohan was knocked to the ground.

"Sneaky little creatures, aren't you?" he said, and rolled out of the way just as two phookas leaped at him from either side. The two charging phookas smashed heads and fell to the ground, dazed.

Rohan stepped toward his sword, but three more phookas raced at him. Scrambling up the wall a few feet, Rohan launched himself at the beasts, knocking them down with his body.

As he reached for his sword, however, a phooka kicked it away. The magical weapon was now beyond Rohan's grasp.

Rohan stood and placed his back against the side of the pit. Two more phookas charged straight at him. He dove out of the way at the last second, and the phookas crashed into the wall. Rohan's dive brought him over to his sword, which he picked up and pointed at the pit's side.

Flames leaped from his sword. Dirt, roots, and rocks tumbled down upon the phookas, burying them.

Firing his mystical sword also broke Maeve's evil spell, and in a flash Rohan was transported back to the castle wall.

Turn to page 10

"Very well," agreed Rohan reluctantly. "A short rest it is, but only a short rest."

Ivar nodded, then stretched out on a patch of fallen leaves and closed his weary eyes. His companions sat down too, breathing a sigh of relief at the brief pause in their journey.

"Do you think he really knows where he's going?" whispered Rohan when he was sure that Ivar had fallen asleep.

"He seems like a trustworthy fellow to me," replied Angus softly. "And you know what a good judge of character I am."

"I notice your judgment of character hasn't kept you out of jail!" Rohan joked.

Angus flashed his pixielike smile, shrugged, and stretched out on the ground.

Next to him, Ivar slowly drifted into a deep, troubled sleep. The lines between the waking and dream worlds blurred. In his dream he walked through the same forest they now traveled, so he was not quite sure whether he was still awake. He was lost, wandering through a thick mist.

Then something moved in the mist. Fear gripped Ivar as he drew his sword.

"Who is there?" he shouted at the vague figure, close enough now so he could hear it growling and snorting.

Maeve's hideous Ogre stepped from the mist and peered down at Ivar menacingly! The enormous beast stood twelve feet tall. The sight of its powerful, muscled body sent shivers through Ivar and he instantly wanted to flee. The creature's horrible twisted face stared right at the young traveler.

Maybe I can frighten him away if I strike first, thought Ivar through his paralyzing fear. Forcing himself to move, he thrust forward with his sword, but the weapon of steel was no match for the towering beast made from dark magic. The Ogre knocked the sword away from Ivar with a casual swat of its hairy hand.

Unarmed, Ivar had no choice but to run through the thickening mist, his anxiety and sense of dread growing with each step. The Ogre followed, surprisingly swift for a creature of his size, matching Ivar step for step.

Ivar's escape ended suddenly when he smashed into the sheer face of a cliff wall. He was trapped. There was nowhere left to run. He spun around just in time to see the grinning, drooling Ogre move in for his final attack. Ivar could smell the beast's hot, foul breath as he closed his eyes tightly and waited for the end.

Ivar bolted upright, waking from his terrible dream, his body covered in a cold sweat. Seeing that he was safe among his companions, he leaped to his feet.

"Are you all right?" asked Rohan, rushing to Ivar's side.

"Maybe resting wasn't such a good idea, after all," Ivar announced, wiping the sweat from his forehead. "Let's move on and find that fairy mound."

Turn to page 20

"Nice try, Maeve," shouted Rohan. "But I know that if I am to one day wear that armor, I will have to earn it." Then he turned his full attention to the battle at hand. "Surround the Ogre!" Rohan hollered to his friends.

Angus, Deirdre, and Ivar spread out. Having the four heroes on all sides confused the beast and divided his attention. The Ogre raced forward, toward Rohan, with his fist raised to strike.

The four heroes aimed their magical weapons. "Now!" Rohan barked out.

Rohan's blazing Sword of Kells let loose a fiery burst.

Angus tossed his Terra Mace. It flew through the air at the Ogre.

Ivar fired a bolt of lightning from his Barbed Trident.

Deirdre unfurled a spinning whirlwind at the creature from her Whirlwind Crossbow.

Rohan's flames engulfed the Ogre. Ivar's lightning and Angus's mace disintegrated him into a pile of dust. Then Deirdre's whirlwind carried the dust away, scattering it over the countryside.

Watching from a nearby crest, Maeve seethed with rage. "This is not the end," she vowed. "I will return with more powerful creatures and finish what I have started. The Kingdom of Kells will be mine!" Then she and Torc turned and rode away.

Turn to page 80

In his magical chamber in King Conchobar's castle in the Kingdom of Kells, Cathbad the Druid worked quickly. His long gray hair and beard shook back and forth as he moved his head. His eyes reflected the wisdom of his years. His simple robes spoke of his humble position. Cathbad was putting the finishing touches on a mixture of powdered flowers and herbs. Standing next to him was his teenage apprentice, Rohan, a strong lad, whose chestnut-brown hair framed his handsome face of fine features and bold, dark eyes.

"Queen Maeve has arrived in Kells to sign the peace treaty with King Conchobar," said Cathbad, as he added a final powder to his mixture. "The war could be over today!"

"Maeve agree to peace?" replied Rohan, studying his master's every move. "Something's amiss. I don't trust her."

"I myself will be attending the meeting, Rohan," said Cathbad. "As soon as I finish with this." Cathbad took a handful of the mixture he had created and tossed it into the air.

Rohan watched in astonishment as the tiny grains of powder transformed into the flickering image of a Phantom Warrior.

The warrior—a seven-foot-tall skeleton—was clad in shining black armor which protected its arms, chest, and legs. Its milky white, bony form and visible skull sent a shiver down Rohan's spine. Upon the Phantom Warrior's head rested a black metal helmet from which two sharp silver fangs jutted. The huge, ghostly warrior pulled out a long, gleaming sword.

"By Daghda!" exclaimed Rohan.

"Test it out, Rohan," instructed Cathbad.

Rohan drew his sword just as the Phantom Warrior thrust his weapon at the young apprentice. Rohan dodged the blow, ducking out of the way. Then he plunged his sword into the warrior's armor. The image shattered into a million tiny fragments, dissolving into the dust from which it was formed.

Cathbad sighed with disappointment. "I'm still unable to mentally control the illusion for more than a moment," he explained.

"Or perhaps I'm just very swift with the sword!" replied Rohan, a smile spreading across his face.

"Let's see how swift you are in cleaning up this mess," shot back Cathbad, nodding his gray-haired head at the cluttered, jumbled chamber. "The time has come for me to go. The king's meeting is about to begin."

Cathbad pulled the hood of his robe over his head and strode away.

A few seconds later a scruffy-looking nineteen-year-old scrambled into the chamber through a window. His thick, black hair flopped into his pixie-like face. His eyes gleamed with a mischievous glow. He pushed the hair from his eyes and greeted Rohan with a hearty handshake. "I thought that old druid would never leave," said the young man.

"Angus, if Cathbad knew a pickpocket was in his chamber . . ." began Rohan nervously.

"What would he do, turn me into a toad?" asked Angus. He began to pull various powders off the shelves. "I can do better magic than that old hawk!"

"You'd better stop!" Rohan warned as Angus began mixing the powders in a bowl. "Only Cathbad knows how to use those." Rohan sighed deeply. He knew better than to argue once Angus got an idea into his head. The two had known each other since the age of six. They'd fought the first time they met. Then, discovering that they both excelled at swordplay, their respect for each other grew and they soon became friends for life. They spent their youth playing in the streets of the village until Cathbad made the young, orphaned Rohan his apprentice. Practicing swordplay for hours on end, by the age of thirteen Rohan and Angus were unbeatable in the village.

"I know what I'm doing," said Angus confidently. He dumped his tenth ingredient into the big wooden bowl.

The mixture bubbled, then exploded in a cloud of rainbow-colored smoke. A horrible smell filled the chamber. The two friends raced out into the castle hallway—where they ran right into Princess Deirdre, the king's eighteen-year-old daughter, knocking her to the cold stone floor!

Deirdre's tall, slender form was clothed in a flowing blue royal gown. Her light brown hair was tousled from the fall, but her delicate, soft face still radiated a regal beauty despite her annoyance with the young men now standing over her.

"Excuse me, princess," said Rohan, offering his hand to help Deirdre up.

"The lovely princess prefers my steady hand," said Angus, reaching down while pushing Rohan aside with his hip.

Before the princess could say a word, a castle guard spotted Angus. "You there, thief! Get over here!" shouted the guard.

"I must be off," Angus said to Deirdre, flashing her a self-confident smile. Then he turned and dashed down the hall with the guard pursuing close at his heels.

"Is that horrible smell coming from you or your friend?" asked Deirdre, getting to her feet.

"Just a small magical mishap," said Rohan, revealing a broad smile of his own. "I can show you how it was supposed to work."

"I have no time to waste on an incompetent apprentice . . . or a thief," Deirdre replied. "I'm on my way to an important meeting with my father. You'd better clean this stinky mess up before Cathbad returns." Then she rushed off, leaving Rohan still smiling after her.

Turn to page 39

In his throne room, King Conchobar conferred with Cathbad.

"You must have powers that can counter Maeve's evil magic!" exclaimed Conchobar to his trusted advisor.

"She has tapped into powerful dark sorcery, Your Majesty," replied Cathbad. "Her conjuring is beyond my means, and I fear her powers will grow stronger yet."

An injured Kells soldier stumbled into the throne room then. His clothes were ripped and he was badly beaten. "My king," began the soldier, struggling to speak. "A huge monster attacked us all." Before he could continue, the soldier collapsed.

"You haven't even begun to see what I'm capable of, Conchobar!" shrieked a voice from behind the king. Everyone in the throne room turned and stared in horror at Maeve, who stood alone in a corner of the room.

"Seize that venomous witch!" ordered Conchobar.

But when the king's guards tried to grab the evil queen, they passed right through her, grasping nothing but the thin air of her illusion.

"It's a spirit from the Otherworld!" cried a guard.

"You will surrender all of Kells to me," said Maeve calmly. "If you do not, I will unleash the full power of my sorcery and Kells will be destroyed. The choice is yours!" Then the image of Maeve faded from view.

King Conchobar's face hardened, but Cathbad could see the worry in his old friend's eyes. "Can we win?" the king asked his advisor. "Is there any way we can stop her?"

"There may be one last hope, my king," replied Cathbad, stroking his long beard thoughtfully. "Long ago the wee folk of Tir na Nog foretold of a great warrior named Draganta, who would bring peace to Kells for a hundred lifetimes. It is written in the Ancient Scroll."

"But that scroll is only a legend," interrupted another of the king's advisors. "It doesn't exist!"

"I can't rely on fairy tales to save my kingdom," said Conchobar sadly. "And I can't send my warriors into battle only to face certain defeat. I have only one choice." He sighed deeply. "Kells must surrender!"

Turn to page 2

The young warriors pressed on, despite feeling tired, and a short while later Ivar led Rohan and Angus into the Boyne Valley. The bright full moon illuminated the eerie grouping of mounds, giving it the creepy feel of a graveyard. Atop a mound in the center of the grouping sat a carved stone symbol.

"Of all the wonders!" said Rohan, excitedly rushing to the mound. "The symbol from my dream!"

"I brought you where you wanted to go," said Ivar. "Now take me to my thief."

As Angus struggled for a reply, Rohan put his finger to his lips. He had spotted a mysterious cloaked figure who had followed them to the valley. "Quiet," he ordered in a hushed voice. "I think maybe your thief has found *you*, Ivar. Perhaps Angus and I can repay our debt."

With only a glance to Angus, the two friends set out in opposite directions, doubling back and sneaking up on the stranger. At a silent nod from Rohan, the two friends jumped the cloaked figure from behind.

Although it was two against one, Rohan and Angus had a tough time wrestling the stranger to the ground. After a difficult struggle, Rohan wrapped his arms around the stranger's waist, while Angus kicked the figure from behind. Rohan pulled the hood off the stranger, only to reveal the extremely agitated face of Princess Deirdre.

"How dare you kick a princess!" shouted Deirdre, getting to her feet and brushing herself off.

"Sweet Lugh!" exclaimed Angus, quite embarrassed. "How was I supposed to know it was you?"

"Who is this girl?" demanded Ivar.

"She is the daughter of King Conchobar," replied Rohan sternly, staring at the princess. "Under strict orders from her father not to join us on this quest."

"You call this a quest?" asked the princess, her voice filled with fury. "Chasing after fairy mounds when Kells is at war! My father was wrong to send a boy to do a warrior's job!"

Before Rohan could respond, the earth beneath them began to rumble.

"What's happening?" shouted Angus as the carved stone atop the mound glowed a bright red. Smoke rose from the mound, and the shaking of the earth grew more violent.

The mound opened up and the four travelers plunged into a huge tunnel. Down they tumbled through the swirling mist, descending at blinding speed toward the very center of the earth.

Rohan, Angus, Ivar, and Deirdre landed on a soft bed of moss in a mixed-up tangle of arms and legs.

"I must be dead!" yelped Angus. "It's the only possible explanation."

Rohan slapped his friend playfully on the back of the head. "Feel that, did you?" he asked.

"Aye!" replied Angus, annoyed.

"See, you're not dead, then, are you?" stated Rohan, smiling. He got to his feet along with the others and looked around in awe. They were in a small cave in an underground world of rocky tunnels, passageways, and caverns.

"By Daghda!" Rohan exclaimed. "This must be the world of the fairies, the wee folk."

"Tir na Nog," said Deirdre, still not quite able to believe that they had found the underground land of legend.

"Interesting," stated Ivar flatly. "Now how do I get out of here?"

"We can't leave now," explained Rohan. "We're

here to find the warrior Draganta. We need him to save Kells."

"*You* may need him," said Ivar. "All *I* need is a way out."

Rohan led Angus and Deirdre down a large passageway. Ivar set out in the opposite direction.

"We really should all stick together," Rohan called after Ivar. "You never know what might be lurking in the dark in a place like this."

Ivar smirked, then disappeared into a dark, narrow tunnel.

"I guess *we'd* best be on our way, then," Rohan said to Angus and Deirdre. As they began to hike deeper into the passageway, a loud growl bellowed from the dark tunnel behind them. A terrified Ivar came racing back toward them, large flames licking at his heels.

"You're right," he said to Rohan. "We should stick together. You might need me."

The others all smiled and continued down the large passageway.

Angus stepped up next to Deirdre. "Take my arm, princess," he offered, extending his arm to her. "I'll lead you."

"I think she would prefer *my* assistance, Angus," said Rohan, approaching the princess from the other side.

Deirdre rolled her eyes and pushed past both Rohan and Angus, taking the lead herself. "I don't need any assistance," she remarked. "Especially from the likes of you two!"

Ivar smiled. Rohan and Angus exchanged dirty looks. Then the group continued along the rocky path.

As they entered a large cavern, Angus raced to the front of the group. After a few seconds he dropped to his knees. "Nobody move!" he shouted.

The others froze in fear.

"Angus!" Rohan called, a wave of panic spreading throughout his body. He dashed toward his old friend.

"What is the danger?" Ivar shouted as he and Deirdre ran after Rohan, the three of them approaching Angus in alarm.

When they reached him, they found Angus kneeling over a huge pile of gold coins. "Aye, a sight it is!" he exclaimed happily. "Now I know why I'm here!"

"Gold, is it?" shouted Rohan, annoyed at his friend. "That's what made you cry out?"

The others glared angrily and shook their heads at Angus for having alarmed them.

Angus glanced up from the gold and saw a tiny man with a white beard and a pointy red hat staring at him and smiling. Other small folk, the fairies of Tir na Nog, raced into the cavern and surrounded the four travelers. The fairies laughed and danced around them in a circle.

"Wee folk of Tir na Nog," announced Rohan. "I am Rohan of Kells. We are here to—"

Rohan was interrupted by a large net falling onto the four young adventurers. The laughter of the fairies grew louder and more ominous as Rohan and the others tried in vain to free themselves from the trap.

Turn to page 52

With a pang of sadness at giving up all that gold, Angus did what he knew was the right thing. He decided to help his friends safely cross the stone path. "The leprechaun told me that it's safe to walk on the green stones, but to stay off of the red ones," he explained. "I trust the wee fella. I'll lead the way."

Angus stepped onto the first green stone. The cavern began to rumble and the green stone sank swiftly, lowering Angus down into a pit at the deepest, darkest depths of Tir na Nog.

"Angus!" shouted Rohan from above, but there was nothing he could do for his friend, who quickly disappeared from sight.

"The leprechaun lied!" snarled Angus when his descent had come to a stop. "He figured I'd not betray my friends and that I'd lead them onto the green stones, thinking they were safe. Turns out I'm the one who was tricked. Now I'm trapped down here." Angus glanced around and quickly realized that his problems were even worse. He was surrounded on all sides by a group of spriggans!

Upon seeing Angus, the horrible creatures inflated themselves into monstrous forms. Their misshapen green heads grew to the size of boulders. Their slime-covered bodies oozed a thick, green, foul-smelling liquid that trailed behind them as they ran toward Angus.

And I thought they were nasty when they were small! thought Angus as the creatures, now twice his size, attacked. He dove to the side and rolled along the cold stone ground to get out of the way of the first wave of giant spriggans. Rising to his feet, Angus drew his sword and swung at the terrifying creatures, who scattered in all directions.

At least this will buy me some time, Angus thought. *Although I can't scare them off forever. There are just too many of them. Sooner or later they'll outflank and overtake me. I've got to move!*

Angus raced down a tunnel as fast as he could, trying desperately to escape the spriggans. He stopped short at the edge of a crevice. He considered leaping across, but it would be a big leap and he wasn't sure he could make it. Turning right, he ran down a passageway. Behind him, he heard the sounds of the spriggans regrouping and following, coming closer and closer. *I don't have much time!* Angus realized. *They'll be on me any minute!*

He kept running and soon came upon an ancient silver mine. From the dust and cobwebs that covered everything, Angus could tell that the mine had been long abandoned. Still, veins of sparkling silver ran through the rock. Large pieces of mined silver were strewn all around. An idea flashed in his mind. He grabbed a long, flat piece of highly reflective silver and raced back to the crevice.

The sound of the clattering, snarling spriggans filled the cave. Fighting the fear welling up inside him, Angus took a running start and leaped across the crevice, just barely making it. He set the long piece of mirrorlike silver on the far side of the fissure, then leaped back across. This time he fell short, but managed to catch the near edge with his fingers. Mustering all his strength, he pulled himself up to the ledge and hid directly across from where he had set up the piece of silver.

When the spriggans arrived, they saw what they thought to be Angus, taunting and making faces at them from across the crevice. What they really saw, however, was Angus's reflection in the silver.

Enraged, the spriggans attempted to leap across the wide fissure. Most didn't make it. The ones that did crashed into the piece of silver and tumbled back into the crevice. All the spriggans soon had fallen to their doom, deep within the earth.

Angus sighed deeply. "Now all I need is a way back up to my friends," he said to himself.

As if he had spoken a magic word, a section of rock slid away, revealing a narrow, winding stone staircase leading up.

"Now how did I do that?" Angus asked himself. "All I said is that I wanted to get back to my friends."

The rock doorway slid closed.

"Hmmm," muttered Angus, scratching his head. "I think I'm on to something here." He paused, then simply stated the word "friends." The doorway reopened, revealing the stairs.

So "friends" is the magic password with this hidden door! he thought, not wanting to speak the word aloud again. *Shows a nice spirit, it does.* Then he raced up the stone stairway. Within minutes he had rejoined the others.

"Sweet Lugh!" said Rohan as Angus stepped out of another hidden doorway beside the other heroes. "It's so good to see you alive, lad!"

Turn to page 54

A disappointed Deirdre rushed off to her room. She flopped onto her bed in frustration. The royal canopy bed was draped in the finest of fabrics. Pure silk hung from the sides of the canopy in a scalloped pattern. Where fringe had once been along the wavy edge, now hung thin crystals. The delicate fingers of glass caught the light and shattered it into a rainbow of colors that danced on the walls of the bedroom. The beauty of her surroundings gave the princess little comfort.

Father is always trying to protect me like some fragile doll, thought Deirdre as she tossed and turned in the bed. *But I'm every bit the warrior that Rohan is.*

She sighed. *I know Father has only my best interests and the best interests of the kingdom in mind, but every fiber of my being tells me to go join Rohan on his quest. Still, I've never disobeyed Father in the past, and I don't think I should start now. He's a kind and wise man, and I would never want to disappoint him.*

Thoughts of Rohan's quest and the future of her father's kingdom filled her head as she lay awake wishing there was something she could do to change the terrible fate that was about to befall Kells.

Sleep finally took her, and Deirdre drifted off into a terrible dream. She dreamed that Queen Maeve had won the war and taken over the entire island.

"Lock them in the dungeon!" shrieked Queen Maeve in Deirdre's dream. Maeve looked on and laughed as her guards tossed King Conchobar and the princess into a dark, cold dungeon and chained them to a dank stone wall.

"Father, are you all right?" Deirdre cried.

"I'm sorry, Deirdre," Conchobar said sadly. "My troops did all they could, but without the warrior Draganta, they were no match for the Temran soldiers."

"This can't be happening!" shouted Deirdre as she dropped to her knees and began to sob. "Let us out!"

"Oh, I'll let you out," cackled Maeve. "To work as my slaves!" Turning to her guards, she shouted orders. "Put the two of them to work in the morning carrying stones to fortify the south wall of my castle. Good night, Your Majesty!" Maeve laughed in a high piercing voice. Her horrible, deafening laugh echoed in the dungeon and crowded everything else out of Deirdre's mind.

"HA! HA! HA!"

The heavy steel door of the dungeon slammed shut, and everything went black and silent.

Princess Deirdre awakened in a panic, bolting upright in bed, covered in cold sweat. She clutched her stomach, which ached as if she had been kicked in the gut. The sound of Maeve's evil laughter and the clang of the slamming dungeon door lingered in her ears.

"Father," she muttered softly, "I cannot let this happen. I am sorry to disobey you, but I know what I must do!"

Then she quietly rushed from the comfort and safety of her room out into the blackness of night.

Turn to page 72

33

Rohan's quest was going none too well. Back in Tir na Nog, he, Ivar, Angus, and Deirdre were tightly bound by brightly colored ropes. They were being led through a tunnel by a group of fairies.

"There's been a mistake," said Ivar as he shuffled along with the others through the underground tunnels. "I'm not with them. I'm here by accident."

"Aye, me too," added Angus.

"Be quiet, you two," whispered Rohan. "I'm thinking of a plan to get us out of here."

"What is it?" asked Deirdre excitedly.

"Well, truth be known, I haven't quite thought of it yet," replied Rohan.

Deirdre sighed. "That's comforting," she said as the group moved on.

The fairies led the four adventurers through

a narrow archway and into a huge cavern. Looking around, Rohan and the others saw that this was no ordinary cave. Wee folk of all kinds stood at attention, staring at the captives. Magnificent tapestries hung from the walls, all trimmed in gold. Mountainous piles of gold coins filled every corner. Centered along the back wall of the cavern was a huge throne, carved from a single piece of white rock, big enough for a human. There was no doubt in the minds of the four travelers that this was a royal court. But whose throne room was it? And was the king or queen good or evil?

"Of all the wonders!" exclaimed Rohan, taking in the majesty of the room.

"This place is unbelievable," added Ivar, turning his head left and right.

"Look at the gold," said Angus, whose eyes focused on the tall piles of coins and little else.

"Silence!" shouted a royal guard. "His Majesty, King Fin Varra, ruler of Tir na Nog, approaches!"

King Fin Varra entered the throne room. Although he was the same size as the rest of the wee folk, his regal manner instantly set him apart. Fine purple robes flowed around him. Upon his head sat a jeweled crown of solid gold. In his right hand he clutched a carved wooden scepter topped by a golden dragon's head. A white beard covered the king's face, giving him a fatherly appearance. The stern look in his blazing eyes, however, told the four friends that their situation was serious indeed.

"Who dares enter the Kingdom of Tir na Nog?" bellowed Fin Varra, stopping at the foot of his human-sized throne.

Deirdre spoke up at once. "I am Princess Deirdre of Kells," she said softly but firmly. "I demand that you release us at once!"

Fin Varra's expression softened. He chuckled and nodded his head. Suddenly the ropes that bound the four travelers peeled off magically, spinning each of the would-be heroes like string around a top. They all landed on the ground with a thud.

"Nice trick," whispered Angus as they got to their feet. "A lot of magical power for such a wee king."

"Why do you invade my kingdom?" asked Fin Varra.

Rohan stepped forward. "Your Majesty, I am Rohan," he began. "I search for the warrior Draganta. My most urgent quest has led me here."

"Aye," added Angus. "And you're supposed to help us."

The king's eyes widened and took on their stern look once again. "We do not help invaders," he said sharply. "We punish them!"

"Our kingdom may soon be conquered by an evil queen," pleaded Rohan.

"This is not my concern," replied the king.

"Your Majesty, if this entire island is ruled by Queen Maeve, then everyone will suffer," explained Deirdre. "Humans and fairies alike."

Fin Varra walked around the four friends, looking them over. He spoke as he walked. "I know of all this," he said in a gentle voice. "It would give me no small pleasure to see Maeve and that dark fairy Mider defeated. The warrior Draganta, who you seek, can do this, as the legends have foretold."

Deirdre's eyes lit up. "Then you'll help us?" she asked.

"How do I know *you* are the ones chosen by the prophesy to find Draganta?" asked Fin Varra.

"Do you recognize this?" asked Rohan, showing the king the birthmark on his arm.

Fin Varra's eyes narrowed as he studied Rohan's mark intently. Reaching into a satchel behind his throne, he pulled out a piece of an ancient scroll and unrolled it. The four travelers stared in wonder at the scroll. It too contained the identical mark, just like the scroll Cathbad had shown Rohan.

"You hold the other part of the legendary scroll!" exclaimed Rohan. "We have indeed come to the right place!"

Fin Varra eyed Rohan warily. "Perhaps you are the chosen one," the king said cautiously. "But perhaps not. Before I give you my help, the four of you must first prove yourselves worthy by passing a test."

"And if we fail this test?" asked Angus nervously.

"Then you'll all spend eternity as spriggans!" answered the king. He pointed with his scepter to a group of hideous, grotesque creatures crawling in the corner of the throne room. They skittered across the stone floor like giant roaches, fighting each other for crumbs of food.

Angus gulped. "I'm sorry I asked!"

Just then a small fairy flew over to Rohan. "I am Aideen, and I warn you, go no further," she whispered as she flitted around his head. Aideen had been secretly watching the young warrior since he'd arrived in Tir na Nog. She had developed quite a crush on the handsome apprentice. "I fear that you will not pass Fin Varra's test, and you will be turned into a spriggan!"

"We will succeed, Aideen," replied Rohan. "Have no fear. My greater concern is for how King Conchobar's army is faring against the forces of Queen Maeve. Will you go find out for us and report back to me?"

Aideen nodded, then flew off on her mission.

Rohan turned his attention back to Fin Varra.

"So, when does this test begin?" he asked.

"It just did!" replied Fin Varra.

The floor beneath the four adventurers dropped open.

Turn to page 42

In King Conchobar's throne room of simple wood and polished stone, the atmosphere was friendly, but tense. Cathbad sat next to the strong and handsome King Conchobar on one side of the long table. Across the table sat the dark and mysterious Queen Maeve, ruler of Temra. Her black robes flowed to the floor, and her dark eyes were narrowed in deep concentration.

Next to the queen sat Torc, her trusted Chief of Guards. Torc, a large, bearded brute of a man, was clad in armor from head to toe. His long sword hung from his armor, at the ready. Two ram's horns curled from his gleaming helmet, giving the tall warrior an even more dangerous appearance.

In addition, leaders of various Kells battalions stood around the room, eyeing the queen and Torc warily.

Princess Deirdre arrived and took a seat near her father.

"A toast!" announced Conchobar, standing and lifting a silver cup filled with nectar. "After ten years of bitter war between our two kingdoms, I congratulate you, Maeve, on our peace treaty."

"And I congratulate you, Conchobar," Maeve replied. "We are both certainly getting what we deserve."

Before anyone had a chance to take a sip, a Kells soldier burst into the throne room. He grabbed the table to keep from falling over, obviously exhausted from battle. A startled murmur spread through the room.

"I bring word of great urgency from the Kells-Temra border, my king," said the soldier breathlessly. "Three Temran battalions tried to sneak across the border to stage a surprise attack. Your soldiers are now defending the border, fighting the Temran troops." Then the soldier collapsed to one knee, the color draining from his scarred face.

King Conchobar stared at Queen Maeve, his eyes burning with fury. "So the treaty was just a distraction!" he shouted angrily.

"I told you, I intend to get what I deserve," snarled the evil queen. "Your ancestors stole Kells from Temra. I will rule this entire island. It is my birthright!"

"Guards! Arrest them," ordered Conchobar. "Now!"

The king's guards drew their swords and moved swiftly toward Maeve and Torc.

"You have no idea of the power I now wield," said Maeve, an eerie calmness in her voice. "The end of your kingdom is near."

Smoke began to rise around Maeve. Just as the king's guards reached her, she and Torc vanished in a flash of lightning. Everyone in the room gasped.

"My king," began Cathbad, the concern showing in his voice. "If Maeve resorts to the dark powers of sorcery, Kells is doomed!"

Turn to page 46

Rohan, Deirdre, Angus, and Ivar tumbled into a deep pit, landing hard on the bottom.

"What did I land on?" Angus asked. He peered underneath him and spotted the bones of a human skeleton. "Ahhh!" he shouted, scrambling quickly to his feet.

Looking around, the others all discovered that the floor of the pit was littered with skeleton bones.

"I wonder what happened to them," Ivar said.

"Maybe they failed the test," replied Angus anxiously.

A loud grinding noise filled the pit. The far wall began to move toward them.

"I think this answers your question, Ivar," said Deirdre with panic in her voice. "Rohan, do something!"

The wall was closing in on them quickly. In a

few minutes they would all be crushed.

Rohan swiftly drew his sword from its sheath and placed the hilt against the moving wall. In a matter of seconds the moving wall pushed the point of the sword against the far wall. The moving wall stopped, but Rohan's sword began to bend from the strain of holding it back. It was clear that the sword would not hold for long.

"Over here!" shouted Angus. "I've found a way out." Angus pushed aside a loose stone, revealing a small passageway out of the pit. He and Deirdre scrambled through the opening.

"I can't move!" shouted Ivar in terror, just as Rohan was stepping through the hidden exit. "My sleeve is stuck between the walls!"

Rohan dashed back toward Ivar. His sword was now perilously close to snapping.

"It's too late!" shouted Ivar. "There's nothing you can do! Save yourself!"

Rohan braced his back against the moving wall, then kicked his sword free. It clattered across the stone floor, stopping at Ivar's feet. "Cut yourself free!" called Rohan, struggling with all his strength to stop the wall's forward movement.

Ivar reached down, picked up the sword, and cut himself free.

"Go!" yelled Rohan.

Ivar raced out of the pit.

Rohan could no longer hold back the wall. He released it, then dove through the small opening, just as the moving wall slammed against the opposite one.

"By Daghda, that was close, it was!" said Rohan when the group was reunited in a narrow passageway.

"You risked your life for mine," said Ivar, stepping up to Rohan and handing him back his sword. "In my country such sacrifice and bravery demands repayment. I'm forever in your debt."

"Help us save Kells and the debt is forgotten," responded Rohan.

"I swear it!" said Ivar, shaking Rohan's hand.

Then Aideen returned from her mission to the world above and flitted over to the group. "I'm afraid the news is dire, Rohan," she reported. "Things are not going well for the king's army. Look." Although she was not among the most powerful fairies, Aideen did possess some magical powers. She moved her right hand in a circular motion. Within seconds a glowing round portal opened in the air, revealing a scene on the battlefield of Kells. The portal showed King Conchobar's soldiers being badly beaten by a troop of Temran warriors.

"They need your help," Aideen said to them. "You can go directly to the battlefield using my magic, simply by stepping through this portal."

Great Seer of Tir na Nog, your powers are needed once again to guide the fate of our heroes.

Should the four heroes go through the portal to the battlefield to try and help the Kells soldiers?

If so, turn to page 64

Should the four heroes continue in Tir na Nog on their quest to prove their worth to King Fin Varra and find the warrior Draganta?

If so, turn to page 49

Seconds later Maeve reappeared in her own throne room. The room's high ceiling and craggy stone walls gave the place the feel of a huge cavern. The walls seemed to move with swirling patterns of spirals and curves. Maeve walked quickly to an elaborately carved table in the center of the room. On it sat a jeweled silver chalice.

Maeve reached her hand up to a burning torch that hung from the throne room wall. A green flame leaped from the torch and danced on her open palm. She carried the magical flame over to the silver chalice and placed it in the center of the jeweled cup.

"Mider, dark fairy, I summon you," she chanted.

The flame died down and a small figure dressed in green appeared in its place. Mider, the evil fairy, looked up at the queen. "Why do you call Mider?" the dark fairy asked her. "You have your magic. Our bargain is finished."

"The powers you gave me are no longer enough," replied Queen Maeve. "I need more dark magic."

"Mider can grant what you desire," said the evil fairy. "For a price."

"No cost is too great to reclaim my kingdom," Maeve declared.

"Very well," said Mider. "It is done."

A flash of bright green flame surrounded Maeve. When it was gone, an ancient rune stone rested atop her ram's head staff. The jagged, translucent stone glowed bright green.

"This stone will give you the power to command greater dark energies," explained Mider.

"And the cost?" asked Maeve.

"Mider shall collect his payment . . . in time," replied the dark fairy as the bright green flames returned, surrounding him. A brilliant burst of green light enveloped Mider, then disappeared. He was gone.

Maeve collapsed to the floor, the energy drained from her body. The queen then felt a new burst of evil power growing inside her. She got to her feet, renewed by the dark energy coursing through her veins. "Forces of dark sorcery, send me a creature!" she chanted as lightning shot from the stone on her staff.

The force of the lightning knocked Maeve against the wall. She looked up, barely able to catch her breath.

Standing before Maeve was a giant Ogre. The massive beast towered over her, standing more than twelve feet tall. Its hairy body rippled with bulging muscles as its hideous face peered down at the queen.

"You serve me?" Maeve asked cautiously.

The Ogre grunted, dropped to one knee, and bowed before its master.

An evil smile spread across Maeve's face. "Go destroy Kells!" she shouted. Then her evil laughter filled the throne room.

Maeve's Ogre tore a path of destruction through Kells unlike anything anyone had ever seen. The giant monster ripped roofs off houses and stomped entire villages into rubble. The villagers fled in terror from the rampaging creature. The brave soldiers of Kells were powerless to stop the devastation of the brutal beast.

Turn to page 17

The four warriors marched on through the narrow underground passageways, ducking to avoid stalactites and stepping around stalagmites as they traveled. After a few minutes, Angus lagged behind, distracted by a gold vein running through a cave wall. He reached out to touch the ribbon of gold, and an invisible force pulled him right through the wall!

"What in the name of Daghda!" he yelped as he magically passed through the solid rock, emerging in a chamber filled with gold. Angus stared at the piles of gold around the room with his jaw gaping open and his eyes afire. He looked down and spotted a tiny leprechaun.

"If it's gold that's got your eye, lad, then I've got a deal for you," said the leprechaun.

"A deal?" replied Angus, glancing at the gold again, then shifting his attention back to the tiny man before him. "Is this some sort of fairy trick?"

"No trick, lad," answered the leprechaun. "Your friends will soon come to the Tomb of Two Stones. The trail of green stones is safe. The red stones spell doom to any who step upon them. Convince your companions to walk on the red stones and the gold is yours!"

Angus slipped back through the magical wall and raced off to catch up with the others. "You'll never believe what I found," he said excitedly when he reached his friends at the Tomb of Two Stones. The wide pathway stretching out before them was made up of alternating red and green round rocks.

"Let me guess," replied Deirdre. "More gold."

"No," said Angus. "I mean, yes, I did find gold, but I also found a leprechaun. He explained to me about these green and red stones. Some are safe to walk on, but some are not."

Suddenly, panic raced through Angus's mind. *I can't betray my friends*, he thought. *Still, all that gold would be nice. But what if the leprechaun was lying? What should I do?*

Great Seer of Tir na Nog, the time has come once again for you to use your power to control the fate of our heroes.

Should Angus trust the leprechaun and lead the others to the green stones, giving up the gold?
If so, turn to page 26

Maybe that leprechaun wasn't telling the truth! Maybe the green stones are dangerous and the red stones are safe! Should Angus suggest stepping on the red stones to the others?
If so, turn to page 54

Back in King Conchobar's throne room, Cathbad arrived with bad news. "I've searched the stars, Your Majesty," reported the druid, "and I've found no trace of Rohan or Angus."

"Right from the start I doubted this plan would work," replied the king.

Cathbad looked around the room, stalling. "There is more bad news," he stated finally. "Your daughter Deirdre is missing. I fear she has joined them."

Shock registered on Conchobar's face, then anger. "I have always trusted your druid powers, as well as your wise counsel, Cathbad," the king said. "But now I have lost not only my kingdom, but my daughter as well!"

Cathbad hung his head sadly.

At the same time, in Maeve's castle, the evil queen moved pieces on a magical chess board. The pieces represented the soldiers of Kells and Temra. Maeve slid a battalion of Temran troops forward, capturing a squadron of Kells warriors.

"My Ogre continues to break through the Kells lines of defense," she said to Torc.

"My soldiers have captured all of Kells up to the Stone Valley," Torc reported. "Almost all of Kells is now in your hands, my queen."

"I will finish taking what is rightfully mine," snarled Maeve. "Begin the final assault on Kells . . . now!"

In a small village near the Stone Valley in Kells, Maeve's magical Ogre continued his rampage. His huge, muscular body tore through everything that stood in his way. Small thatched huts that were the homes of the villagers were crushed with a single blow from his powerful fists. Wagonloads of food were overturned. Trees were even ripped from the ground and used as weapons against the soldiers of Kells. Things looked bleak. Now, more than ever, the future of Kells depended on the success of Rohan's quest.

Turn to page 33

54

"I don't think that leprechaun can be trusted," said Angus. "I think we should step on the red stones. I'll lead." Angus placed a foot onto the first red stone. He shifted his weight onto the foot and stood fully on the stone. Nothing happened. Letting out a deep sigh of relief, he led the others safely across the Tomb of Two Stones, stepping only on the red, round rocks.

"Which way now?" asked Deirdre.

Rohan looked around. They had entered a sandy chamber that appeared vaguely familiar. "This place is a maze," he said. "It looks like we're back where we started."

"Either you're getting taller, Ivar, or I'm getting shorter," observed Angus. He looked down and realized that he was sinking into the sandy floor.

"I can't move my legs!" shouted Deirdre.

"By Daghda!" exclaimed Rohan. "It's quick-sand. And we're all sinking!"

"It's been nice knowing you, Rohan," said Angus. "You've been a good friend, lad."

"I wish I had more time to get to know all of you," added Ivar. "But it looks like our time is up."

"I'm sorry, princess," said Rohan as they all sank up to their waists. "I've failed you and your father."

"Now Kells is doomed, as surely as we are," said the princess.

Then the four friends disappeared below the surface of the quicksand.

Turn to page 59

56

"I can't risk the lives of my people on a druid's apprentice!" Conchobar said in frustration, glaring at Rohan and Cathbad, who stood before him in the king's throne room.

"The warrior Draganta can save your people," pleaded Rohan. "And I am the one to find him!"

"Father," began Deirdre, who was standing, as usual, beside the king. "If this boy says he can find Draganta, then let him try."

"'Boy,' is it?" said Rohan angrily. "I'm a man. And I won't 'try' to find Draganta, I *will* find him!"

"My king," began Cathbad in a calm voice. "You have trusted my advice in the past. Trust it now. It may be our only hope."

The king thought for a moment, then sighed deeply. "You may go, Rohan. But if you have not succeeded by the Summer Solstice, Kells will have no choice but to surrender."

"Aye," said Deirdre, turning to Rohan. "When do we leave?"

"Your intentions are noble, Deirdre," said the king sternly. "But a quest of this nature is too dangerous. I forbid it!"

"As you wish, Father," replied Deirdre. Then she turned and left the throne room.

Turn the page

Great Seer of Tir na Nog, the time has come for you to use your power to control the fate of our heroes.

Should Deirdre obey her father?

If so, turn to page 30

Should Deirdre sneak out of the castle later tonight and join Rohan on his quest?

If so, turn to page 72

Down the heroes plunged, through a tunnel. They landed on a bed of soft moss—in Fin Varra's throne room!

"We're still breathing!" Ivar shouted with glee as the four got to their feet and brushed themselves off.

"The test is over," said Fin Varra, appearing before them.

"Then we've passed," said Deirdre in a hopeful voice. "We've proven ourselves worthy of your help."

"Passed!" exclaimed Fin Varra. "It's failed, you have, and it's spriggans you'll be!"

A magical mist suddenly surrounded the four warriors.

Deirdre stepped forward, struggling through the thick cloud. "If you dare to turn a future queen into a spriggan, so be it," she stated. "But

I demand you spare the others. They are here only to help save Kells. At least let them return and try to help my father defeat Maeve."

Fin Varra nodded and waved his hand. The magical mist swiftly disappeared. The four friends stood stunned. "You have indeed passed my test, warriors," said Fin Varra. "You, Rohan, demonstrated courage by rescuing Ivar from the moving wall. Angus, you showed honesty by turning down the leprechaun's gold to save your friends' lives. And Ivar, you showed loyalty to Rohan after he saved you.

"I was only waiting for Deirdre to show a noble trait, which she has just done with her unselfish offer. You have all proven yourselves worthy. Now here is what I promised."

Fin Varra reached into his satchel, pulled out his scroll, and handed it to Rohan. The young warrior unrolled the yellowed parchment. But as he scanned it, his expression quickly turned sour.

"But this is only one more torn section of the entire scroll," he said, disappointed. "Where's the rest of it?"

"You now have all you need to lead you to the warrior Draganta," explained Fin Varra as the others examined the new piece of scroll. "Summon the powers of the elements and behold your arsenal!"

Each, in turn, recited a magical chant read from the Ancient Scroll.

"Fire within me!" shouted Rohan. As he spoke the words, the image of a suit of gleaming red-and-gold armor appeared before him and floated in the air just above his head.

"Earth beneath me!" yelled Angus, and a shining silver suit of armor appeared, taking its place beside Rohan's.

"Water around me!" chanted Ivar. He watched in awe as a blazing blue suit of armor magically joined the others in midair.

"Air above me!" called Deirdre. A dazzling suit of white armor appeared, completing the image that floated before them.

"Sweet Lugh!" exclaimed Rohan. "It is the armor I saw upon the four great warriors in my dream. And such magnificent armor it is!"

A powerful roar filled the throne room. All eyes turned to the image of a huge and mighty dragon.

"Pyre, the Fire Dragon of Dare, will be your ally," explained Fin Varra. The fairy king waved his hand and the images of the armor and the dragon vanished like smoke in the air. "What you have just seen are visions of things to come. You must find the four suits of armor and the dragon yourselves. That quest will lead you to the great warrior who can save your people."

"But good king, my father's castle is threatened," pleaded Deirdre. "The end of Kells is near. We need your help *now*!"

"You will not leave Tir na Nog unaided," Fin Varra assured them. He made a magical gesture, and three magnificent weapons floated into the room. This time they were not merely ghostly images, but real things!

The Whirlwind Crossbow—a long shaft with a curved bow supporting a taut string—floated across the room and landed in Deirdre's hands.

The Terra Mace—a steel handle attached to a heavy chain with a craggy rock on the end—drifted over to Angus.

Finally, the Barbed Trident—a long scepter decorated with a dragon's head and wings, ending in a three-bladed crest—made its way through the air and came to rest in Ivar's hand.

"Of all the wonders!" exclaimed Angus as the three warriors examined their fine new weapons.

"And what of my weapon?" asked Rohan.

"You, my lad, have had it all along," replied Fin Varra. "Strike your sword against my throne."

Rohan touched the blade of his old rusty sword against the gleaming white throne of the king of the fairies. Blinding white energy flashed from the throne and traveled all the way up the sword to the hilt, transforming the dull blade into a powerful, shimmering, magical weapon— the legendary Sword of Kells!

"By Daghda!" exclaimed Rohan, examining the magnificent weapon in his hand. "Now this is how it's supposed to look!"

Aideen flew into the throne room and zipped over to Rohan's ear. She had been keeping track of events in Kells and now spoke in desperate, urgent tones. "You must hurry," she said. "Your king's castle is under siege!"

Rohan turned to Fin Varra. "These weapons are truly marvelous, Your Majesty," said Rohan. "But we need Draganta!"

"Use what I have given you," replied the fairy king. "If you win this battle at the castle, then you can quest for the great warrior to bring lasting peace to your kingdom. Now go, before it is too late!"

Turn to page 67

64

"**I** must help the king's army or all is lost," said Rohan.

"I'm with you," added Ivar loyally.

"We don't know if this Fin Varra will really help us anyway," Angus pointed out.

"My father's army needs all the soldiers they can get to battle the Temran troops," Deirdre said.

"Then it is decided," said Rohan. "We will use your magical portal, Aideen, and help the king's army!"

One by one the four young warriors stepped through the portal. In the blink of an eye they were magically transported to the battlefield in Kells.

Drawing their swords, they rushed into the fray.

Rohan engaged a Temran soldier. He swung his sword, but the blow was blocked by the

Temran's shield. Four more Temran soldiers joined their comrade. One of the new arrivals swung a mace at Rohan, who ducked into a crouch to avoid the blow. Another Temran charged right at Rohan, his sword gleaming. Rohan sidestepped the charging soldier, then stuck out his leg and tripped him. The soldier toppled to the ground. *I'm greatly outnumbered*, thought Rohan, retreating. *I can't keep this up forever!*

Angus battled two Temran soldiers. One wielded a long sword, the other a dangerous dagger. The first soldier brought his sword down toward Angus, who dove to the side, rolling out of the way. The dagger-wielding soldier was upon him in a flash. Angus grabbed his wrists, then used his legs to flip the Temran over his head. Leaping to his feet, he saw three more soldiers rushing toward him. *I may be a good fighter, but* that *good, I'm not!* Angus thought, slipping behind a huge tree for cover.

Ivar swung his sword at a Temran, who met the cold steel with a blazing blade of his own. Metal clanged against metal as the two fought fiercely. Ivar heard a Temran soldier sneaking up behind him. He swiftly sidestepped the newcomer, then engaged him in skillful swordplay. *Two against one is not so bad*, he thought, brandishing his sword against his enemies. Then three more Temran warriors came charging right at him. *Five against one, however, are not odds I care for!* He turned and ran to find Rohan.

Deirdre also battled bravely. She wielded her sword powerfully against a Temran soldier, but he countered with a savage swing of his own, knocking the sword from her hands. Deirdre turned and dashed away, and soon caught up with Ivar.

"How did you fare?" Deirdre asked breathlessly as they ran.

"About the same as you, from the looks of things," replied Ivar, also out of breath.

"Hey! Wait for me!" called Angus, joining the others as they passed by the tree that had given him momentary protection.

They soon caught up to Rohan. "We're hopelessly outnumbered," he shouted as the four heroes retreated toward the glowing portal. "There are just too many Temran warriors. We cannot turn the tide of battle here. We must stay true to the quest and bring back the warrior Draganta. He is our only hope."

"No argument here," said Angus.

The others nodded in agreement, then the four warriors stepped back through the glowing portal—which on this side showed an image of Tir na Nog—and instantly returned to the kingdom of the fairies to resume their quest.

Turn to page 49

Back in Kells, King Conchobar's castle was under heavy attack. On a nearby hillside, Queen Maeve sat upon her majestic black steed. She watched as her troops got the better of the Kells soldiers, who they greatly outnumbered. Torc, her Chief of Guards, sat atop his horse beside her.

"Victory is nearly yours, my queen," said Torc confidently.

"It is guaranteed," replied Maeve.

On the castle wall King Conchobar himself battled a Temran soldier. But for each soldier he beat back, two more instantly took his place. The desperate king glanced up toward a nearby hilltop and spotted four figures racing toward the castle. He recognized three of the four rushing to join the fray as Rohan, Angus, and Deirdre.

"Deirdre!" he shouted. "Go back! All is lost here!"

But the four warriors ignored the king's warning. Carrying their newly acquired weapons, they rushed into the heart of the battle.

A swarm of Temran warriors surrounded Ivar at once. He aimed his Barbed Trident at the group. A bolt of lightning shot from the trident, scattering the Temran soldiers. "Thank you, wee folk!" said Ivar, discovering the power of his new weapon.

Angus immediately focused his attention on a group of Temrans who were firing huge rocks at the castle from a catapult. He swung his Terra Mace over his head three times, then released it. As the magical weapon soared through the air, the rock on its chain grew in size until it was as big as a boulder. The huge boulder landed on the catapult, smashing it into pieces.

"Sweet Lugh!" exclaimed Angus. "Now this is my sort of weapon!"

Nearby, another group of Temran warriors raced toward Deirdre. "I hope Fin Varra was right about this weapon," she muttered to herself, then aimed and fired her Whirlwind Crossbow. A huge gust of swirling air shot from the magical crossbow, knocking over the charging Temran soldiers. "At last, a weapon that can help my father save his kingdom," remarked Deirdre.

Up on the castle wall things got worse in a hurry for King Conchobar. Two more Temran soldiers joined the two he was already battling. Rohan quickly rushed to the king's side, forcing back the two new attackers.

Eight more Temrans swarmed toward the king and Rohan, who pointed his enchanted Sword of Kells at the onrushing soldiers. Its gleaming blade changed into a spear of fire. The flaming blast sent the Temran soldiers running.

From his vantage point high on the castle wall, King Conchobar saw that the rest of Maeve's forces were retreating, fleeing from the four young warriors' mystical powers.

Afterward, when the four friends had gathered in the castle, the king asked, "Where did you get such weapons?"

"The wee folk of Tir na Nog gave them to us to help defend Kells," replied Rohan.

Cathbad the Druid rushed onto the castle wall in a panic. "The battle is far from over!" he exclaimed. Moments later, the king and the four warriors found out exactly what he had meant.

The huge, horrible head of Queen Maeve's Ogre rose into view. The hideous beast leaped onto the castle wall and charged at the heroes, grunting and snarling.

At that moment a suit of gleaming red-and-gold armor appeared before Rohan, hovering in the air. It was the same armor he had seen first in his dream and later in Fin Varra's throne room.

Great Seer of Tir na Nog, for one final time your power and judgment are needed to guide the fate of our heroes.

Should Rohan grab the armor to see if it can help him battle the Ogre?

If so, turn to page 5

Should Rohan fight the Ogre without the armor, using only the weapon given to him by Fin Varra?

If so, turn to page 10

The next day, Rohan went to the local jail, where he found his best friend Angus relaxing on the floor of a stone prison cell.

"They caught me stealing purses," explained Angus, "and they put me in here."

"Well, I can get you out," offered Rohan. "If you help me."

"And what kind of help might that be, lad?" Angus asked suspiciously.

"I'm going on a quest," Rohan answered proudly. "To find the warrior Draganta who was spoken of in the Ancient Scroll as the one who could save Kells. They told me I could ask anyone I liked to join me on the quest. So, I'm asking you. Interested?"

"Risk my life on a quest or rot in jail," began Angus. "Tough choice there."

"I could probably do it myself," said Rohan, starting to walk away.

"Hold on, friend!" called Angus. "A quest it is! Now get me out of here!"

That afternoon Rohan and Angus stood in the castle's courtyard. Cathbad joined them and handed a shoulder bag to Rohan. "Just some supplies you might need, lads," said the druid. "Though I'm still not certain this quest is the best idea."

"We'll be fine, Cathbad," said Rohan, clasping his mentor's shoulders. "And thank you. For everything."

Cathbad smiled, but then his face turned serious. "Follow the foot path to the Boyne Valley— land of the fairy mounds," he advised. "From there you may be able to enter Tir na Nog."

"And what then, once we're inside Tir na Nog?" asked Rohan.

"I wish I knew," replied Cathbad. "Tir na Nog is where my piece of the scroll came from. You might get help there finding the rest of it . . . but only if the wee folk of Tir na Nog find you worthy. Keep in mind, lad, that the fairies who live there are not human. Some have dangerous magic."

Rohan nodded. "Then we're off," he said, embracing his mentor. "Goodbye, Cathbad."

"Good journey, apprentice," called out Cathbad, who watched as Rohan and Angus set off on their quest.

After hiking until dusk, the two friends made camp deep in the forest. "Get some rest," Rohan told Angus. "You'll need it."

Both travelers soon drifted into deep sleep.

Rohan fell into a fog-shrouded dream. In his dream the dense forest was obscured by the mist that drifted among the trees and swirled along the ground. Rohan squinted at a small figure that floated toward him through the fog, trailing golden light behind her.

"Chosen One, heed my words," said the glowing figure, who now revealed herself to be a magical fairy. "A stranger you'll encounter will lead you to Tir na Nog, the land of my people."

As the fog swirled around him, a series of wondrous images danced before Rohan. The visions were shrouded in mist and unclear, but they filled Rohan with wonder nonetheless. He saw a carved stone symbol atop a fairy mound, and then caught a quick glimpse of a stranger.

"If you prove yourself worthy to the wee folk," continued the fairy in the dream, "armor and weapons, the likes of which you've never seen, will come to you. You will meet a dragon, and the warrior Draganta atop a horse."

A dragon roared and three armored figures stepped from the fog. Standing off to one side a fourth armored figure—Draganta—sat atop a mighty steed. Then the dream abruptly ended.

Rohan sat up and opened his eyes. The fog, the fairy, and the wondrous images were all gone. Only the eerie night sounds of the pitch-black forest remained. He glanced at Angus, who slept soundly beside him. Then Rohan stretched out and tried to fall back asleep, both excited and disturbed by the visions in his dream.

In the morning the two friends broke camp and continued on a path through the forest. As they walked, Rohan told Angus of his dream.

"The dream is a sign, it is!" said Rohan, with great excitement in his voice.

"Aye, a sign it is," repeated Angus. "A sign you ate too many gooseberries before going to sleep last night!"

Without warning, a large tree limb next to the path snapped up into the air. Rope attached to the limb snagged Rohan and Angus, and in a flash the two travelers found themselves dangling upside down in the air, their legs caught in the rope.

"Looks like I've captured a couple of rogues," said a young man as he stepped from the forest thicket. He was simply dressed in the clothes of a traveler. A hood dangled from the back of his loose-fitting shirt.

"Cut us down," insisted Rohan. Then he recognized the man as the stranger from his dream!

"Let's see if either of you is the gentleman I seek," said the stranger, peering at the faces of his captives.

Rohan reached for his sword. "Hang on," he whispered to Angus, then cut the two of them down. Landing hard on the ground, the two friends leaped to their feet. They waved their swords and advanced on the stranger, who pulled out his own sword.

Steel clashed against steel as the stranger struggled to hold his own against two opponents. Angus and Rohan were both superb swordsmen who had been battling as a team since childhood. The two friends spread out. Rohan approached the stranger from his left, Angus from his right. Angus moved quickly toward the stranger, his sword extended. The stranger backed away to his left, where Rohan was waiting. A swift slash from Rohan's weapon flung the sword from the stranger's hand.

"Gentlemen, I meant you no harm," said the stranger, his hands raised over his head in defeat. "I am Prince Ivar from the land beyond the sea. A jeweled silver chalice—a valued treasure of my realm—was recently stolen. All I know of the thief is that he has a scar on his forehead and that he lives on this island. But I am now satisfied that neither of you is the thief."

"Imagine mistaking *me* for a thief," said Angus, winking at Rohan. They both lowered and then sheathed their swords.

At which point Rohan remembered his dream. "Do you know of a fairy mound with a carved stone symbol atop it?" he asked Ivar.

"Perhaps," Ivar replied cautiously. "Why?

"Help us find the fairy mound and we'll help

you get your chalice back," Angus blurted out. "I know this scoundrel you're looking for."

"Agreed!" said Ivar excitedly. "I'll lead you to the mound. Follow me."

As they followed Ivar, Rohan whispered to his friend, "You don't really know the thief he's seeking."

"Aye," replied Angus, a mischievous light shining in his eyes. "But my little fib got us on our way, didn't it!"

Rohan shook his head as they continued to follow Ivar into the woods.

Unknown to the three travelers, a mysterious cloaked figure peered around a tree, watching them. The cloaked stranger now followed them as they journeyed farther into the forest.

After hiking for most of the day, Ivar grew tired. He had been traveling through the forest for several days now and weariness was beginning to catch up with him. Every bone in his body cried out for him to take a break.

"I must rest," Ivar said, stopping to catch his breath.

"We can't spare the time," replied Rohan. "Every minute we lose brings Kells one step closer to defeat. We must press on."

"I have been traveling alone for days," explained Ivar. "My sleep has been fitful at best, leaving one eye open at all times to search for danger. I ask you to allow me just a few hours sleep before we press on."

Rohan thought for a moment. *Ivar certainly is insistent, and I could use a little nap myself. Perhaps his story is true, but dare I trust a total stranger enough to let down my guard and sleep?*

Great Seer of Tir na Nog, once again you must use your wisdom and power to control the fate of our heroes.

Should the travelers stop to rest? If so, turn to page 7

Should the travelers press on and go directly to the fairy mounds? If so, turn to page 20

The next day a joyful celebration was held in King Conchobar's throne room. Rohan, Angus, Ivar, and Deirdre stood proudly before the king.

"You have saved our kingdom and our honor," Conchobar proclaimed. "Kells will be forever in your debt."

Cathbad, beaming with pride, gazed at his young apprentice. Rohan had come a long way from the clever, skillful youngster he had taken under his wing all those years ago. Ever cautious, though, the wise druid offered words of advice. "Mind you, Rohan, there's little time. Maeve is still very much a threat. She will no doubt try to increase her dark powers."

"Cathbad is right," said Deirdre. "Even our magical weapons won't be enough when she attacks again. We must find the mystical armor and Pyre, Fire Dragon of Dare, to aid us."

"We must then quest for the warrior Draganta," added Rohan. "For only then will Kells be at peace."

"Then quest you will," announced the king. "With my blessing. Let this victory be only the beginning."

Turning to face his court, Conchobar added, "I give you . . . the Mystic Knights!"

Rohan, Deirdre, Angus, and Ivar joined hands and raised them above their heads. The four heroes all smiled as a deafening roar of applause exploded from the court.

The saga of the Mystic Knights continues in Book #2, *Fire Within, Air Above!* Don't miss the magic!